Sammy's Great Escape

PICTURE WINDOW BOOKS
a capstone imprint

This book is dedicated to Steve Blunt. You let me play music with you and it's even more fun than being a famous lion trainer!-Marty

Molly Mac is published by
Picture Window Books
A Capstone Imprint
1710 Roe Crest Drive
North Mankato, MN 56003
www.mycapstone.com

Education Consultant: Julie Lemire
Editor: Shelly Lyons
Designer: Ashlee Suker

Library of Congress Cataloging-in-Publication Data
Names: Kelley, Marty, author, illustrator.
Title: Sammy's great escape / by Marty Kelley; illustrated by Marty Kelley. Description: North Mankato, Minnesota: Picture Window Books, a Capstone imprint, [2017] Series: Molly Mac Summary: When Molly volunteers to look after Sammy McHamsterhead, the class pet, for the weekend she has visions of training him to do tricks and becoming rich and famous-but when she leaves the cage open and Sammy escapes she realizes that she has to find him or confess her carelessness to her teacher, Mr. Rose. Identifiers: LCCN 2016043045
ISBN 9781515808350 (library binding)
ISBN 9781515808398 (paperback)
ISBN 9781515808435 (ebook pdf)
Subjects: LCSH: Hamsters-Juvenile fiction. Responsibility-Juvenile fiction. Humorous stories. CYAC: Hamsters-Fiction. Pets-Fiction. Lost and found possessions-Fiction. Responsibility-Fiction. Humorous stories. LCGFT: Humorous fiction. Classification: LCC PZ7.K28172 Sam 2017 DDC [E]-dc23

LC record available at https://lccn.loc.gov/2016043045

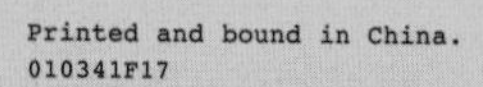

Printed and bound in China.
010341F17

Table of Contents

Chapter 1
Eraser Training 7

Chapter 2
Top Hats and Hamster Tails 11

Chapter 3
Lots of Glitter 18

Chapter 4
The Disappearing
Sammy Trick 22

Chapter 5
What's That
Squeaking Sound? 33

Chapter 6
We Need Some Green Goo . . . 40

Chapter 7
Silly Squirrel Squares 46

TASCO
CAT

All About Me!

A picture of me!

Name: Molly Mac

People in my family:
Mom
Dad
Drooly baby brother Alex

My best friend: KAYLEY!!!!

I really like: Crunchy delicious tacos! But not if they have tomatoes on them. Yuck! They are squirty and wet.

When I grow up I want to be: An artist. And a famous animal trainer. And a professional taco taster. And a teacher. And a super hero. And a lunch lady. And a pirate!

My special memory: Kayley and I camped in my yard. We made s'mores with cheese. They were surprisingly un-delicious.

Chapter 1

Eraser Training

Ffffft. Fffffft. Fffffft.

Molly pushed her eraser back and forth across her desk. "Roll over," she said. "Come on, boy. Roll over."

Kayley sat down next to her. "Molly Mac?" she asked.

"Don't ask," replied Molly.

"I'm asking," Kayley said.

"Last night, we watched a TV show about circus animal trainers," Molly said. "I want to be a rich, famous animal trainer. But my parents won't let me get a pet lion. Do you think there are any rich, famous eraser trainers?"

"Probably not," Kayley said.

"Then I can be the first!" Molly picked up her eraser and dropped it in the middle of her desk. "Play dead," she demanded.

The eraser didn't move.

"See? I'm great at this!" Molly said. "I'll be rich and famous and have my own TV show!"

"Do you think people will want to watch a show about you training an eraser to play dead?" Kayley asked.

Molly sighed. "I guess not," she said. "That's why I really need a pet lion. My parents keep saying no for some reason."

Mr. Rose walked to the front of the room. "Good morning, class," he said. "I have some special news today. I need some help."

Molly jumped to her feet. "Do you want me to call 9-1-1?" she asked. "I know their phone number! Well, most of it, anyway."

"No, Molly," Mr. Rose said. "I don't have an emergency. I just need a little help. I need someone's family to take care of our class pet for the weekend. I'm going away this weekend. I can't take Sammy McHamsterhead with me."

Molly Mac jumped to her feet and waved her arms, "**ME! ME! MEMEMEMEMEEEE!**" she yelled. "**OOOOHHHH, PLEEEESE pick me! PICK ME! PICK ME! PICK ME! ME! MEEEE!**"

Mr. Rose asked Molly to please sit down and stop yelling. "I'll call your mother and make sure it's all right with her, Molly," he said.

"**Yessss!**" Molly pumped her fist. "I'm going to be a rich, famous animal trainer after all!"

Chapter 2

Top Hats and Hamster Tails

Molly Mac sat down next to Kayley at lunch that day. "Do you have a top hat I can borrow?" she asked.

"Why do you need a top hat?" Kayley asked.

Molly opened her lunch box. "Because I'm going to be a rich, famous animal trainer," she replied. "And animal trainers always wear top hats. Everybody knows that."

"Why do they wear top hats?" Kayley asked.

"Because they want to look fancy for the animals," Molly explained. "Animals don't do tricks for people who dress like slobs."

"Why didn't you need to wear a top hat to train your eraser?" Kayley asked.

"Erasers have lower standards than animals," Molly told her.

Kayley chewed a bite of sandwich. "Hmmmm. . .," she said. "That makes sense, I guess. But what about the animals? Don't they want to look fancy, too?"

"I never thought of that," Molly said.

Mr. Rose walked by the table carrying his lunch tray.

Molly jumped up and grabbed his arm. "Mr. Rose! Mr. Rose!" she shouted. "Do you know what size top hat would fit Sammy McHamsterhead?"

Mr. Rose took a deep breath. He let it out slowly. "Do I even want to know why you're asking me that, Molly Mac?" he asked.

"Probably not," Molly replied. "Can we just pretend I never asked?"

Mr. Rose nodded. "I think that might be the best idea," he said. "I called your mother about watching Sammy this weekend."

"**Yay!**" Molly cried. "I'm so excited to watch him!"

Mr. Rose shook his head. "Sorry, Molly," he said. "I'm afraid that your mother said no. I'll have to find someone else to watch Sammy."

★ ★ ★ ★ ★

After school, Molly ran through the front door. She pulled out her sketchbook. "I made a list of reasons why you should let me watch Sammy this weekend," she said to Mom. "Sit back and relax while I read them to you."

"Okay," replied Mom. "Go ahead, Molly."

Molly opened her sketchbook and started reading. "Reason number one: Sammy McHamsterhead is very cute. He doesn't smell very bad most of the time. Reason number two: I will look very good in a top hat."

"That's true, Molly," said Mom.

"Reason number three: I can take care of Sammy. I will show you that I can be responsible. Then you will let me get a pet lion because nobody wants to watch a trained eraser. Reason number four: Mr. Rose needs help. You always say that we should help people whenever we can."

Molly closed her sketchbook. "So?" she said. "Can I **PLEASE** watch him this weekend?"

Mom smiled. "You know what, Molly?" she replied. "You're right."

"I am?" Molly asked. "Wow, how in the world did that happen?"

"I do always tell you that we should help people," Mom said. "Mr. Rose needs help. We can watch Sammy for the weekend. You will also see what a big responsibility pets are."

"So we really can watch him?" Molly asked.

"Yes," Mom said. She stood up and walked toward the phone. "I'll call Mr. Rose right now."

Molly jumped up and hugged Mom. "**Thank you! Thank you! Thank you!**" she shouted. "I'll have Kayley come over for the weekend to help. It will be like two helpers for the price of one! You will see how responsible I am with Sammy. Then you will definitely let me get a pet lion!"

Chapter 3

Lots of Glitter

Ffffft. Shhhhhk. Ssssst. Ssssst.

That Saturday morning, Molly was hard at work in her room. She was cutting and gluing. She was taping and twisting and glittering.

Sammy McHamsterhead was scampering around in his cage on the desk next to her.

Kayley walked into the room. She was carrying her sleeping bag. She also had her stuffed dog named Herman. "Hi, Molly!" she said. "Wow! Look at all that glitter. It looks like a unicorn farted in your room!"

"I hope I used enough," Molly told her.

"I think you did, Molly," said Kayley.

Molly held up a red piece of paper. A cloud of rainbow glitter drifted to the floor. "You can't be a rich, famous TV star without lots of glitter. Everybody knows that."

Kayley tossed her things onto Molly's bed.

Molly wiped her hands on her pants. More glitter fluttered to the floor. She opened the door of Sammy's cage. She carefully reached in. "Are you ready to start training, Sammy?" she asked.

Molly patted Sammy gently on the head. He squeaked a tiny hamster squeak and pooped. Molly pulled her hand out of the cage and pointed. "Did you see that?" she asked. "He just pooped when I patted his head! That's his first trick!"

Kayley scrunched up her nose. "That's not a trick," she replied. "He poops about a hundred times a day in school. Nobody is going to watch a TV show about a pooping hamster. That's nasty."

"You're probably right," Molly said. She ran back over to her desk. She held up a piece of paper. "I've been working on a list of tricks we're going to teach Sammy."

Amazing Tricks to
Teach Sammy McHamsterhead
1. Jump through a flaming hoop.
2. Walk on a high wire.
3. Do flips on a flying trapeze.
4. Get shot out of a hamster cannon!

"A hamster cannon?" asked Kayley.

"Don't ask," said Molly.

Chapter 4

The Disappearing Sammy Trick

"We have a lot of training to do," Molly said. "But first, we need our top hats!"

Molly held up two paper top hats. More clouds of glitter sprinkled to the floor. "I made a red one for you and a yellow one for me!" she said.

Kayley took the sparkly red top hat and gently placed it on her head. "Wow! It's beautiful!" she replied.

"**And look at this!**" Molly cried. "I even made one for Sammy McHamsterhead!" She held up a tiny blue top hat. "Let's see if it fits!"

Kayley looked at her hat in the mirror. Molly skipped back over to Sammy's cage.

"Does Sammy's hat fit?" asked Kayley.

"I don't know," Molly answered. She pointed to Sammy's cage.

It was empty.

"**He disappeared!**" she cried.

"Sammy escaped from his cage!" Kayley cried.

"Are you sure he escaped?" Molly asked. "Maybe this is just his first big trick. It's The Disappearing Sammy Trick!"

"This isn't a trick," Kayley said. "You left the cage open and Sammy got out!"

Molly looked under her pillows while Kayley looked under the bed.

"He's not here," Molly said.

"He's not here either," Kayley said.

"If we don't find him, my parents will never buy me a pet lion," Molly moaned. "And then I'll never be a rich, famous animal trainer with my own show. And then what will we do with those top hats I made?"

"If we don't find Sammy, Mr. Rose is going to be very upset," Kayley said. "And that's way more important than the top hats."

Molly gasped. "You're right!" she replied. "I wasn't even thinking of poor, old Mr. Rose. We've got to find Sammy."

"Where could he be?" Kayley asked.

Molly pointed at a glittery trail of tiny footprints leading out the door of her room.

"Come on!" Molly said.

Molly and Kayley followed the footprints out into the hall. The trail zig-zagged back and forth across the carpet.

They tip-toed down the hall toward Alex's bedroom.

"Where do you think Sammy could have gone?" Kayley asked.

"Where would you go if you were a hamster?" Molly asked.

Kayley shrugged. "Probably Ohio, I guess," she said.

"Why would you go to Ohio?" Molly asked.

"That's where my grandparents live," Kayley said.

"Do you think Sammy McHamsterhead has grandparents?" asked Molly.

"Maybe he has grandhamsters," Kayley said. "Do you know which state they would live in?"

"Which one?" Molly asked.

"**New Hamster!**" Kayley joked.

Kayley and Molly both laughed.

Molly stopped laughing and pointed to the floor. "**Look!**" she said. "The trail of footprints ends at Alex's door."

Molly and Kayley crept over to the door. It was open half way. They peeked into the room.

Molly held her finger to her lips. "**Shhhhh**. . . Alex is sleeping in his crib," she whispered.

"And he isn't alone," Kayley said. She pointed at Alex. Curled up next to him was a small, furry lump.

"We found Sammy," Molly whispered. "Now we have to get him out of that crib without waking up Alex."

Molly and Kayley crept back to Molly's bedroom.

"Don't worry," Molly said. "I've got a plan."

"That's what worries me," Kayley said.

Molly opened her closet door and dug around inside.

Scrunk. Klunk. Bang!

She yanked open the top of her toy box. Then she dug through the toys piled inside.

Ksssshhhh. Plunk. Chrrrrunk.

She lifted out a long butterfly net, a toy fishing pole, and a dart gun.

"Do I even want to know what you're planning, Molly?" Kayley asked.

"Probably not," Molly said. "Come on!"

Molly carried the net, the pole, and the dart gun down the hall to Alex's door. Kayley crept along behind her.

When they got to the door, Molly handed the net to Kayley. She pointed to Alex. She waved her hands and twiddled her fingers. She made big swooping motions with her arms.

"What are you doing?" whispered Kayley.

"I'm telling you the plan with top secret signals," Molly told her.

"I thought you were dancing," Kayley said. "Can you tell me the plan with less secret words?"

"I'm going to tie the string from this fishing pole to the dart from this dart gun," said Molly.

"Then I'm going to shoot the dart at Sammy. When it sticks to him, I'll pull him over here. Then you catch him in the net. Easy!"

"Maybe we should just tip-toe in and catch Sammy," Kayley suggested.

"Nope," Molly said. "Too risky. We can't wake up Alex, or Mom will be really mad."

She tied the string to the rubber dart. "Get ready with that net."

Molly took careful aim. Kayley raised the net over her head.

Pop!

Molly pulled the trigger. The dart snapped loose from the string and sailed across the room.

The dart landed gently on Alex's head.

Alex sat up and looked around.

The furry lump next to Alex rolled through the crib rungs.

Molly looked over at the furry object. It wasn't Sammy McHamsterhead. It was Alex's stuffed monkey, Mr. Banana Face.

Then Alex started screaming.

Mom's footsteps thumped up the stairs.

"**Uh, oh. . .**" groaned Molly.

Chapter 5

What's That Squeaking Sound?

Molly and Kayley sat in the living room with Dad. Mom rocked Alex back to sleep.

"I can't believe you let Mr. Rose's pet hamster escape," Dad said. "I'm very disappointed in you, Molly."

"It was an accident," Molly said. "I was so excited about his top hat. I couldn't wait to train him to jump through a hoop of fire. I just forgot to lock his cage door."

"You need to find Sammy McHamsterhead," Dad told her. "He's Mr. Rose's pet. You are responsible for him."

"I know," Molly said. "I have a new plan. We can make signs and post them all over the neighborhood. We can offer a million dollar reward!"

"Do you have a million dollars?" Dad asked.

Molly shrugged and shook her head.

"Maybe we can build a trap for Sammy!" Molly said. "We can put a taco under a box. Then we could hold the box up with a stick. When Sammy eats the taco, we pull the string. The box will drop on him."

"Do you have a taco?" Dad asked.

Molly shook her head again.

"What if we build a time machine so we can—" Molly began.

"Maybe we should just start looking for Sammy," Kayley interrupted.

"That's the best idea I have heard yet," Dad said.

Molly and Kayley stood up to start looking.

Dad held up his hand. "What was that?" he asked.

Molly and Kayley froze and listened. They heard a tiny sound coming from the kitchen.

Squeak. Squeak. Squeak.

"**It's Sammy!**" cried Molly

Molly ran into the kitchen and slid across the floor in her socks. "Gotcha!" she yelled.

Dad and Kayley ran in after her.

"Where is he?" asked Kayley.

"I don't know," said Molly.

They froze and listened.

Squeak. Squeak. Squeak.

Molly pointed to a cupboard door that was open. "It's coming from there!" she said.

“He better not be eating all my Organic Wheat Germ Bran Cereal,” Dad said.

Molly slid silently toward the cupboard.

“Get ready,” Kayley said. “Molly, if he runs out, I’ll try to grab him quickly, okay?”

Molly gave her a thumbs up.

Squeak. Squeak. Squeak.

Molly slid closer and closer.

Squeak. Squeak. Squeak.

Molly crouched right next to the cupboard. She carefully reached for the door.

"When I count to three, I'll open the door and grab him," she whispered. "Get ready! One. . .two. . .three!"

Molly yanked the cupboard door open.

SQUEEEEEAAAAAAAK!

The cupboard door squeaked loudly when she opened it. Sammy was not in the cupboard.

Molly wiggled the cupboard door back and forth.

Squeak. Squeak. Squeak.

"It was just the door squeaking," Molly groaned.

"Come on," said Kayley. "Let's go find Sammy."

Chapter 6

We Need Some Green Goo

Molly and Kayley raced from room to room looking for Sammy. They looked under chairs, under couches, and under tables. They looked in closets, in laundry baskets, and even in Molly's sneakers.

"Maybe Sammy got hamsternapped!" said Molly. "Should we call the police?"

"I don't think that's a good idea, Molly," said Kayley. "We need to keep looking."

Molly and Kayley spent the rest of the afternoon searching for Sammy. They did not find him anywhere.

"**Dinner!**" Dad called.

Molly and Kayley climbed into their seats.

"I'm starting to think that Sammy McHamsterhead really disappeared," Molly said. "We can't find him anywhere."

"I'm sure he'll turn up," Mom said. She buckled Alex into his high chair.

"And to cheer you up, I made your favorite dinner," Dad said. "**Crunchy, delicious tacos!**"

"Thanks, Dad," Molly said.

"Thanks, Mr. Mac," Kayley said.

At dinner, Molly snuck a few pieces of taco into her pocket. When she and Kayley went back to her room, Molly sprinkled the taco pieces into Sammy's empty cage.

"Do I even want to know what you're doing, Molly?" asked Kayley as she put on her pajamas.

"I'm leaving a snack here. Maybe Sammy will come back to his cage," Molly said. "**Everybody loves my dad's tacos!**"

Molly and Kayley snuggled into their sleeping bags on Molly's floor.

Molly sighed. "This is bad, Kayley," she said.

"Yup," Kayley agreed.

“We looked everywhere,” said Molly. “Where could Sammy be?”

“Maybe he really went to New Hamster to visit his grandhamsters,” Kayley said.

Molly and Kayley both laughed a little.

“What are you going to do if we can’t find him?” Kayley asked. “Mr. Rose is not going to be happy.”

Molly rolled over. She propped herself up on her elbows. "I've been thinking about that," she said. "Do you think we have time to build a hamster cloning machine? We could make a new Sammy! I saw that in a movie one time. It looked pretty easy. All we need is **green goo** and some science stuff. I have a science kit in my closet. We can mush up some leftover peas to make **green goo**."

"I don't think that's going to work," Kayley said.

"You're probably right," Molly sighed. "Maybe we can go to the pet store and buy a new hamster that looks just like Sammy McHamsterhead. We can put the new hamster in Sammy's cage. Mr. Rose will never know!"

"That doesn't seem very honest," Kayley said. "I don't think we should do that."

"I know," Molly replied. She flopped over on her back. "But I don't want to tell Mr. Rose that I lost Sammy. He'll be so sad."

"Then we only have one other choice," Kayley said.

"Start working on that time machine?" Molly asked.

"No," Kayley said. "We have to find Sammy."

Chapter 7

Silly Squirrel Squares

The next morning, Molly hopped out of her sleeping bag and ran over to Sammy's cage. "Sammy? Did you come back for tacos?" she asked.

"Did he?" Kayley asked. She wiggled out of her sleeping bag. Then she ran over next to Molly.

"Nope," said Molly.

The pieces of taco were still sprinkled across the bottom of the cage.

Molly and Kayley trudged downstairs to get some breakfast.

Neither one of them was smiling.

Dad was sitting at the table sipping his coffee and feeding Alex some applesauce. "How are you two ladies this morning?" he asked.

"Horrible," Molly groaned. "Sammy didn't even come back to his cage for the free, all-you-can-eat taco bar last night. What are we going to do?"

"You're going to keep looking until you find Sammy," Mom said.

Molly trudged to the squeaky cupboard. She swung it open. "What kind of cereal would you like, Kayley? We have Silly Squirrel Squares, Mom's Boring Bran, and Dad's Organic, Sensible Sticks and Twigs."

"**I love Silly Squirrel Squares!**" Kayley cried. "They have a three-week supply of sugar in every bowl. Plus there is a prize in every box!"

"I know," Molly said. "But I'm only allowed to get these when you come over. Maybe you should move in and save me from Boring Bran."

Molly took the box of Silly Squirrel Squares out of the cupboard. The top was torn open. "**Hey! Who's been eating my cereal?**" she asked.

She lifted the torn flap with her finger and peeked into the box.

Squeak!

"**Hey!**" she cried. "I found the prize in the box of cereal. **It's Sammy McHamsterhead!**"

Everyone sat around the breakfast table eating the French toast Mom had made.

"Sorry you didn't get to have Silly Squirrel Squares," Molly said. "But I guess Sammy McHamsterhead likes them even more than you do. He ate almost the whole box."

"Well, he was in the box all night," Kayley said. "And this French toast is way better than cereal."

"Thanks," said Mom. "I'm glad you like it."

Molly put her fork down. She wiped her mouth with a napkin. "Now that we found Sammy McHamsterhead, do you guys think I can finally get a pet lion?" she asked.

"I want to be a rich, famous animal trainer and have my own TV show. I already have a top hat," Molly added.

Suddenly, Alex banged his spoon on the tray. A tiny piece of French toast flew off his plate and plopped right into Dad's coffee.

"**Hey!**" Dad said. "**My coffee!**"

"That was a good trick, Alex," Mom said.

"It **was** a good trick, wasn't it?" Molly said. "Mom, what size top hat would fit Alex?"

"Do I even want to know why you're asking that, Molly Mac?" Mom asked.

"Probably not," replied Molly.

All About Me!

A picture of me!

Name:
Marty Kelley

People in my family:
My lovely wife, Kerri
My amazing son, Alex
My terrific daughter, Tori

I really like: Pizza! And hiking in the woods. And being with my friends. And reading. And making music. And traveling with my family.

When I grow up I want to be:
A rock star drummer!

My special memory:
Sitting on the couch with my kids and reading a huge pile of books together.

Find more at my website:
www.martykelley.com

MORE MOLLY MAC

Meet Molly Mac, the curious girl who is always onto something. She's a whirlwind full of questions, and she's out to find the answers!

MOLLY MAC
The Best Friend Bandit
by MARTY KELLEY

MOLLY MAC
Tooth Fairy Trouble
by MARTY KELLEY

MOLLY MAC
Lucky Break
by MARTY KELLEY

THE FUN DOESN'T STOP HERE!

Discover more at
www.capstonekids.com

- ★ Videos & Contests
- ★ Games & Puzzles
- ★ Friends & Favorites
- ☆ Authors & Illustrators